The history

Author: Goodman, Michael E.
Reading Level: 6.7
Point Value: 1.0
ACCELERATED READER QUIZ# 26001

MICHAEL E. GOODMAN

THE HISTORY OF THE
PIRATES

CREATIVE EDUCATION

Published by Creative Education
123 South Broad Street, Mankato, Minnesota 56001
Creative Education is an imprint of The Creative Company

Designed by Rita Marshall
Editorial assistance by Tracey Cramer & John Nichols

Photos by: Allsport Photography, Focus on Sports, SportsChrome.

Copyright © 1999 Creative Education.
International copyrights reserved in all countries.
No part of this book may be reproduced in any form without written permission from the publisher.
Printed in the United States of America.

Library of Congress Cataloging-in-Publication Data

Goodman, Michael E.
The History of the Pittsburgh Pirates / by Michael E. Goodman.
p. cm. — (Baseball)
Summary: A team history of the Pittsburgh Pirates, who have been playing baseball since the 1880s.
ISBN: 0-88682-921-6

1. Pittsburgh Pirates (Baseball team)—History—Juvenile literature.
[1. Pittsburgh Pirates (Baseball team)—History. 2. Baseball—History.]
I. Title. II. Series: Baseball (Mankato, Minn.)

GV875.P5G63   1999
796.357'64'0974886—dc21   97-6348

9 8 7 6 5 4 3

When you think of Pittsburgh, Pennsylvania, you think of hard work. Mental pictures form of giant factories, glowing steel mills, and sprawling construction sites. It's true that Pittsburgh is one of the hardest-working cities in America. But it is also a city known for its three majestic rivers and the bridges that cross them. It is a place that combines natural and manmade wonders.

The Pittsburgh Pirates baseball teams have nearly always matched the character of their city and fans. Pirates teams have been known for their tough, hard-nosed play for more than 100 years—from the 1880s to the present.

Pittsburgh shortstop Arky Vaughan.

Over the years, the Pirates' many exceptional hitters have captured 24 batting championships, their powerful sluggers have earned 10 National League home-run crowns, and their swift base-runners have garnered 21 stolen-base titles. Many of these hard workers are in baseball's Hall of Fame—from old-timers Honus Wagner, Harold "Pie" Traynor, and the Waner brothers, to Roberto Clemente and Willie Stargell, who starred in the 1960s and 1970s. All told, they helped bring the city of Pittsburgh five world championships, nine National League pennants, and six Eastern Division crowns.

Today, the Pirates' organization is in the process of building Pittsburgh's next great team. Young stars like Tony Womack, Al Martin, Esteban Loiaiza, and Jason Schmidt represent a bright future for a franchise that possesses a glorious past.

On April 15, the Alleghenies, a member of the International Assocation, played their first game at Union Park.

WORKING TOWARD THE FIRST WORLD SERIES

Professional baseball began in Pittsburgh in 1876 when the minor league Pittsburgh Alleghenies were formed. The team joined the National League 11 years later, but had a rough time winning games during its first few years as a major-league club.

The low point came in 1890 when many of the Alleghenies' best players jumped to a rival organization, the Players' League. The team's record fell to a devastating 23–113 that season, sinking it to last place, 66½ games behind the league leader.

The following year, two important things happened. The Players' League disbanded for lack of money, and the Alleghenies earned a new name. Athletes who had jumped to

All-Star catcher Jason Kendall.

Jack Chesbro led the league in shutouts with eight and led Pittsburgh to its first NL crown.

the Players' League in 1890 were expected to return to their old teams in 1891. However, Pittsburgh signed one of the Players' League stars, shortstop Louis Bierbauer, just prior to the 1891 season and refused to surrender him to his former club, the Philadelphia Athletics.

"You've stolen one of our best players. You're no better than pirates!" the frustrated Athletics cried. The Pittsburgh management decided to keep not only the player, but the name as well. From that moment on, the team has been known as the Pittsburgh Pirates.

But even the new name didn't help. The Pirates remained near the bottom of the league until 1900. That was when four teams dropped out of the National League. The owner of one of those clubs, Barney Dreyfuss, bought a part-interest in the Pirates and brought with him to Pittsburgh 14 players from his old team's roster, including future Hall-of-Famers Honus Wagner, Fred Clarke, and Rube Waddell. The influx of talent made Pittsburgh an instant powerhouse. The Pirates captured three straight National League titles in 1901, 1902, and 1903.

Leading the way on those great Pirates teams was the "Flying Dutchman," Honus Wagner. The bowlegged Wagner was an outstanding fielder and hitter. One reporter wrote: "He walks like a crab, fields like an octopus, and hits like the devil."

"Wagner didn't look like a shortstop," teammate Tommy Leach said. "He had those huge shoulders and those bowed legs, and he didn't field balls the way we did. He just ate up the ball with his big hands, like a scoop shovel, and when he threw to first base, you'd see pebbles and dirt and everything else flying over there along with the ball. It was quite a sight! He was the greatest shortstop ever. The greatest everything ever!"

As fine as he was in the field, Wagner may have been even better on offense. During the first decade of the 1900s, he captured eight National League batting titles, five stolen-base crowns, and led the league in slugging percentage twice. He could do it all.

With Wagner, Clarke, and Leach leading the batting attack and pitchers Jack Chesbro, Charles "Deacon" Phillipe, Sam Leever, and Jesse Tannehill starring on the mound, the Pirates were almost unstoppable from 1901 to 1903.

After the team's third-straight National League championship, club president Barney Dreyfuss sent a letter to Henry Killilea, owner of the American League champs, the Boston Pilgrims. "It is my belief that if our clubs played a series on a best-out-of-nine basis, we would create great interest in baseball, in our leagues, and in our players. I also believe it would be a financial success," Dreyfuss wrote.

The Boston owner accepted the challenge, and baseball's first World Series became a reality. Unfortunately for Pittsburgh fans, the Pilgrims, led by the immortal Cy Young, outdueled the Pirates to win the first series five games to three.

Six years later, Pittsburgh won another National League pennant and earned the right to play the Detroit Tigers in the 1909 World Series. Fans were excited about the matchup of two of the greatest players of all time—Honus Wagner of Pittsburgh and Ty Cobb of Detroit.

Wagner outplayed Cobb in the series, but the real hero for the Pirates was a little-used rookie pitcher named Babe

On June 30, the Pirates christened Forbes Field, the first park built completely with concrete and steel.

Following in Wagner's footsteps—shortstop Jay Bell.

Another talented athlete, outfielder Andy Van Slyke.

Adams. Adams baffled the Tigers' batters with his sweeping curveball and won three times to bring Pittsburgh its first world championship.

Pittsburgh fans were on top of the world—but only for a little while. Sadly, it would be 16 long years before the fans would be able to cheer for another champion.

Winning with Pie and "Poisons"

Several things contributed to the Pirates' surprising downfall after the 1909 World Series. For starters, the players became cocky and overconfident after becoming world champs. Then the club began spending huge amounts of money to buy hotshot players who never lived up to their reputations. Finally, the superstars of the previous decade—guys like Wagner—simply got older and slower.

Pittsburgh's fortunes began to change for the better in the early 1920s with the arrival of two fine infielders—shortstop Glenn Wright and third baseman Pie Traynor. These two solidified the Pirates' defense and joined hitting stars Kiki Cuyler and Max Carey to give Pittsburgh one of the best offensive attacks in the National League. Together they brought a league pennant and a world championship banner back to Pittsburgh in 1925.

Probably the most outstanding all-around player on that 1925 team was Traynor. During his career he set a new defensive standard for third basemen that only such future stars as Brooks Robinson, Graig Nettles, and Mike Schmidt have been able to match. "Gosh, how he could dive for those line drives down the third base line and knock the ball

Future Hall-of-Famer Max Carey led the NL in stolen bases for the 10th time in 13 years.

down and throw the man out at first! It was remarkable," said a teammate. Traynor was also a star at bat, hitting more than .300 in 10 of his 13 full seasons with the Pirates.

Traynor was soon joined in Pittsburgh by a new pair of offensive stars—the Waner brothers. As a rookie in 1926, Paul Waner did two important things for the Pirates. He led the team with a .336 average, and he told the team owner, "My younger brother Lloyd is an even better player than I am. You'd better grab him." Luckily, the Pirates took his advice. During the following year and for more than a decade afterward, the Waner brothers were two-thirds of the Pirates' outfield. They earned the nicknames "Big Poison" and "Little Poison" because they were murder on opposing pitchers, combining for more than 5,600 career hits.

Pie and the "Poisons" led the Pirates to another pennant in 1927, but Pittsburgh was no match for the Yankees' "Murderers' Row" of Babe Ruth, Lou Gehrig, Earle Combs, and Tony Lazzeri in the World Series that year. The Pirates lost in a four-game sweep.

Little did Pittsburgh fans know, but that 1927 National League pennant was the last one their heroes would win for 33 years. The Pirates stayed near the top of the league throughout the rest of the 1920s and 1930s, but they just couldn't win it all. "Gee, that was tough to take," Paul Waner said later. "We had good teams, too. You know, Pie, Arky Vaughan, and Gus Suhr in the infield, and Bill Swift, Mace Brown, and Remy Kremer on the mound, and me and Lloyd—all good players. But we never quite made it. It'd just tear you apart."

The near misses tore Pirates fans apart, too. Year after

1 9 3 5

Shortstop Arky Vaughan sported a .385 average, a mark that has been unequalled in the NL since.

Danny Murtaugh led the Pirates to a World Series championship and was named Manager of the Year.

year, the fans hoped for a big winner, but the team never quite reached the top. In fact, the Pirates would hit rock bottom before they rose again.

"MAZ" PERFORMS A MIRACLE

During the 1940s, the Pirates were an average team with one real star—slugger Ralph Kiner, who won the National League home-run title a record seven seasons in a row. But in the 1950s, the Pirates were horrible, losing more than 100 games each year in 1952, 1953, and 1954.

Pittsburgh fans were upset, but not general manager Branch Rickey, who took over the team in 1950. He calmed the fans by announcing that the club was following a five-year rebuilding plan. "We're pointing toward 1955," the optimistic Rickey declared.

He began trading away veterans and bringing in such young players as shortstop Dick Groat, first baseman Dick Stuart, outfielder Bob Skinner, and relief pitcher Elroy Face. In a final brilliant move before the 1955 season, Rickey "stole" a young Puerto Rican star named Roberto Clemente from the Brooklyn Dodgers' organization and brought him to Pittsburgh. Then Rickey retired, certain that his rebuilding program would pan out in the end.

It took five more years, but in 1960, all of the pieces came together. The glue binding the various parts was a tough-as-leather second baseman named Bill Mazeroski. One of the finest-fielding second-sackers of all time, "Maz" was also a solid clutch hitter. And he was a natural team leader, too. A teammate once said, "Maz never came unraveled. There was

Aggressive play is a Pirates tradition.

One of baseball's all-time greats, Roberto Clemente.

always a smile on his face. He never got too high after a victory or too low after a loss. Maz taught me the value of patience and consistency."

Maz's patience and steady play paid off in 1960 when the Pirates captured the National League title by a seven-game margin over the Milwaukee Braves. Maz batted a solid .273 with 64 RBIs. Dick Groat led the league in batting that year, with Clemente close behind. Pirates Vern Law and Bob Friend were among the league's top pitchers, and Elroy Face saved 24 games out of the bullpen.

As fate would have it, the Pirates faced off against the Yankees in the 1960 World Series—just as they had done 33 years before. It was a strange series. Pittsburgh edged by the Yankees to win three of the first six games, while the New Yorkers blew out the Pirates by wild scores of 16–3, 10–0, and 12–0 for their three victories. Everything was riding on the seventh game.

That game was very wild, too; the lead kept switching from one side to the other. First, the Yanks seemed to have a win cinched when they led 7–4 in the eighth inning. But a bad-hop grounder kept a Pirates rally alive, and Pittsburgh scored five times to head into the ninth with a two-run advantage of its own. The Yanks soon wiped that out in the top of the inning, tying the score at 9–9 and setting the stage for a Mazeroski miracle in the bottom of the ninth.

Maz was the first Pittsburgh batter in the bottom of the ninth. He also became the last one, smashing a Ralph Terry fastball over the left-field wall for the series-winning run. Maz, who seldom let his emotions show, danced and leaped all around the bases. Pirates fans also jumped for joy at the

Outfielder Matty Alou captured the league batting title with a .342 mark.

Like Clemente, Dave Parker was a Pittsburgh slugger (pages 18-19).

sweet revenge of beating the New York Yankees for the world championship.

CLEMENTE ENDURES AS HERO

Catcher Manny Sanguillen joined teammates Roberto Clemente, Willie Stargell, and Dock Ellis on the NL All-Star team.

Pittsburgh's time at the top was short-lived. The next year, the team fell to a disappointing sixth place and remained in the middle of the league standings throughout most of the 1960s. Willie Stargell, a future star who joined the team in 1962, said, "The spark had disappeared from the club, and as a result the team of destiny's magic had passed. All that remained were 25 talented ballplayers not good enough to win a pennant."

The most talented player of that group—and the most misunderstood—was Roberto Clemente. A man of great pride and honesty, Clemente's personality sometimes caused him problems with sportswriters and fans. Early in his career, his limited English kept him from speaking with the media, and many reporters took his reluctance to communicate as arrogance. Clemente felt he did not always receive the recognition he deserved for his fine play, and he said so openly. He also had a chronically sore back, and he complained a lot about his aches and pains. As a result, writers and fans criticized him for being a crybaby.

But neither pains nor language problems could keep Clemente from hitting a baseball. He led the league in batting average four times during the 1960s and missed hitting more than .300 only once during the decade. He was also a great right fielder, winning 12 Gold Glove awards. Clemente possessed a cannon for an arm and a flair for the dramatic catch. "Robby's playing today," Pirates pitcher Steve Blass would say, "so there will be peace in right field. He'll catch everything that can be caught."

Clemente finally earned the respect he deserved in the 1971 World Series, when the Pirates took on the Baltimore Orioles. With fans from all over the country watching him on television, Clemente got at least one hit in each of the seven games, batted more than .400, and almost single-handedly led Pittsburgh to the world championship. Not surprisingly, he was a unanimous choice as the Most Valuable Player of the series.

Pirate slugger Willie Stargell finished as the decade's leading home-run hitter with 296.

His comment after the series was misunderstood. He said, "For me, I am the best." Some people thought that he was bragging, but that expression is an old Spanish saying that means "I did the best I am capable of doing." And he did.

Clemente had one more great year in 1972 when he recorded his 3,000th hit. After the season ended, a terrible earthquake occurred in the Central American country of Nicaragua. At home in Puerto Rico, Clemente helped collect supplies and medicine to aid the earthquake victims. He decided to deliver these things personally to make sure they got to the people who needed them most. "No one will steal if Roberto Clemente is there," he said. However, the old plane in which he was flying crashed into the sea during a storm, and Clemente was killed.

At his funeral, the governor of Puerto Rico remarked, "Our youth lose an idol. Our people lose one of their glories." Several months later, in a special election, Clemente became the first Latin American player ever named to baseball's Hall of Fame.

Willie Stargell.

"POPS" STARGELL LEADS PIRATES

With Roberto Clemente gone, the Pirates needed a new leader, and Pittsburgh general manager Danny Murtaugh asked Willie Stargell to become the team's captain. "I'd be honored, as long as you don't expect me to change," the big first baseman responded.

"No, we won't ask you to change," Murtaugh replied. "We like you just as you are."

Stargell was a natural leader who inspired his teammates with his hard work and his great sense of humor. He made a special point of "adopting" such younger players as Dave Parker, Al Oliver, Richie Hebner, Bruce Kison, and John Candelaria to help them adjust to the major leagues. As a result, Parker gave Stargell the nickname "Pops."

Pops Stargell helped create a close-knit Pirates family that started to win big in the late 1970s. In 1979, they rose all the way to the top.

That year, Stargell chose a theme song for the team, a disco tune called "We Are Family." Stargell asked that the song be played at all Pirates home games.

"The song not only brought us and the fans closer together, but it became a rallying cry for the city as well. We were all one—my teammates, our families, the fans, the city, everyone. Pittsburghers all moved to the same beat," the Pirates' captain explained.

That beat was a winning one, as the inspired Pirates edged the Montreal Expos for the Eastern Division crown and then swept the Cincinnati Reds in the playoffs to reach a spot in the World Series.

1 9 8 9

Bobby Bonilla led the Pirates in games played, home runs, hits, RBIs, doubles, and triples.

1 9 9 0

Pitcher Doug Drabek posted 22 victories to lead the National League.

The Pirates' opponents in the series were the Baltimore Orioles, the same team they had beaten for the 1971 championship. Just as in 1971, the series went a full seven games. In that last game, Pops Stargell pounded four hits, including a homer and a double, to lead his family to victory.

BONDS, BONILLA PROPEL PIRATES INTO CONTENTION

In the early 1980s, the family broke up. Willie Stargell retired (and was soon elected to the Hall of Fame), hitting stars Dave Parker and Bill Madlock left for new teams, and top pitchers Bert Blyleven and John Candelaria were eventually traded. The team slowly dropped in the rankings, sink-

Bobby Bonilla, a power threat from both sides of the plate.

ing toward rock bottom in the National League East in 1984, 1985, and 1986.

Like Branch Rickey in the mid-1950s, new Pirates general manager Syd Thrift wasn't worried by the losses. He had a plan in mind. He wanted to rebuild the team with young stars so that the Pirates could become consistent winners.

Thrift started by promoting two young outfielders from his minor-league system, Barry Bonds and Bobby Bonilla. Then he made wily trades for such players as Andy Van Slyke, Doug Drabek, Neal Heaton, and Jay Bell. Thrift asked Pittsburgh fans to be patient while these young players developed.

The fans' patience was soon rewarded. In 1988 the Pirates surprised most people by making a strong run for the National League East title. Sadly, the club faded near the end of the season, and the New York Mets finished atop the division.

After an injury-riddled 1989 season, the Pirates were back in 1990 and better than ever. Pittsburgh jumped out to an early lead in the National League East, slipped behind the Mets, and then wiped out the New Yorkers in two late-season series to grab the club's first division title since 1979. Unfortunately for Pittsburgh fans, the Pirates came up against a sensational Cincinnati Reds club in the 1990 playoffs. The Reds stopped the Pirates in six hotly contested games.

For the Pirates it was a bitter loss, but the stellar play of their outstanding trio of outfielders—Bonds, Van Slyke, and Bonilla—gave hope for the future. Bonds was named National League Most Valuable Player in 1990 when he batted .301, smacked 33 homers, stole 52 bases, and drove in 114 runs. Bonilla was close behind in the voting that year. "I wish I could split the award and give half to Bobby," Bonds

Heavy hitter Barry Bonds drew 32 intentional walks from cautious opposing pitchers to set the Pirates' team record.

Speedy second baseman Tony Womack (pages 26-27).

Shortstop Jay Bell led the Pittsburgh club in batting average (.310) and hits (187).

commented at his award ceremony. "I wish I could share it. To me, he's just as much the MVP as I am."

As good as Bonds and Bonilla were, the honor of best outfielder may have belonged to center fielder Van Slyke, whose presence in Pittsburgh was the result of a big trade with the Cardinals in 1987. His aggressive play earned him the respect of players around the league, but also resulted in several painful injuries that kept him out of the lineup at times.

However, the outfielders weren't the only stars on the 1990 team. "When you're a good club that is not outstanding," manager Jim Leyland said. "There's a chance for everyone to be a hero." Such players as infielders Jay Bell and Jeff King and catcher Mike LaValliere all had heroic moments.

The pitching staff was also revamped entirely. Leading the way were Doug Drabek, the National League Cy Young Award winner in 1990, and Bob Walk.

In 1991, the Pirates again nabbed the NL East title, this time facing the Atlanta Braves for the pennant. With a surprisingly poor batting performance from Bonds, the Pirates' star slugger, the Pirates blew a 3–2 lead to lose the series to Atlanta.

They were back in 1992, once again a force to be reckoned with. In a repeat of the 1991 season, the battle for the league title again came down to the Pirates and the Braves. This time Pittsburgh had its sights set firmly on a World Series.

But for the third-straight year, the Pirates were denied a trip to the Fall Classic. This time the heartbreaking loss occurred in the bottom of the ninth inning of game seven of the National League Championship Series. The Pirates had led 2–0, but the Braves had struck for a run and had the bases loaded.

Up to the plate came seldom-used Braves pinch-hitter Francisco Cabrera. Amazingly, Cabrera singled, scoring two runs—the second on an excruciatingly close call at home plate. The Braves took the final game—and the championship—four games to three. "We were so close," sighed a dejected Bell. "I really can't believe it happened still."

PIRATES REBUILD FOR THE FUTURE

The 1992 loss to the Braves was devastating to the Pittsburgh organization. The team had lost Bobby Bonilla to free agency after 1991, and shortly after the 1992 postseason, the cash-poor Pirates lost Barry Bonds and Doug Drabek as well. Pittsburgh sank to fifth place in 1993 and finished third in 1994.

During the 1995 season, Pirates management continued to be distracted by serious financial problems; there was even talk of moving the Pirates from their historic location in Pittsburgh to northern Virginia. In February 1996, newspaper heir Kevin McClatchy bought the Pirates. He vowed to keep the team in Pittsburgh and to make it competitive again.

However, the 1996 season was still dismal, and McClatchy was forced to slash the payroll at season's end. The Pirates had no choice but to release some of their finest players: pitcher Denny Neagle, who had a 27–14 record over the previous two seasons; Orlando Merced; Carlos Garcia; Dan Plesac; Dave Clark; and Charlie Hayes. Manager Jim Leyland left shortly afterward, resigning in frustration.

Not much was expected from the small-budget Pirates in 1997, but surprisingly, the extremely young club made a

Pitcher Esteban Loaiza won his first major-league start and tied for the NL lead in games started.

Steady outfielder Al Martin provides veteran leadership.

Rising star, outfielder Jose Guillen.

Kevin Young was expected to match or beat his '97 season batting average (.300).

strong showing. Their record of 79–83 surpassed most experts' predictions by 15 to 20 games. Its new manager Gene Lamont coaxed veteran performances from players with very little experience but a great deal of talent and desire. Youngsters like sparkplug second baseman Tony Womack, who hit .278 and led the National League in steals with 60, or 21-year-old outfielder Jose Guillen, who belted 14 homers and drove in 70 runs, complemented veteran outfielders Al Martin and Jermaine Allensworth. "A lot of people thought we would be a joke," observed Womack. "But if we can keep this group of guys together and add another bat or two, we'll be doing the laughing."

The Pirates are also developing a solid pitching staff for the years ahead. Starters Esteban Loaiza, Jason Schmidt, Francisco Cordova, and Jon Lieber all look to have bright futures, and reliever Rich Loiselle posted 29 saves in his first year as a closer. "I like this group of guys a lot," said Lamont. "They're young, but they're dedicated to doing the work it takes to become great."

For Pittsburgh fans, it's hard to imagine a better match for their hardworking city than the hustling, blue-collar Pirates of today. With continued improvement from their young, up-and-coming stars, Pittsburgh appears ready to challenge baseball's elite once again.

DATE DUE		
APR 2 4 2012		
MAY 1 8 2012		

Library Media Center
Renfroe Middle School
220 W. College Ave.
Decatur, GA 30030